The Van

Green Light Readers
Harcourt, Inc.
Orlando   Austin   New York
San Diego   London

The Van

Holly Keller

Sam has a van.

Pam sat in the van.

Max sat, too.

Dan sat in the van.

Pat sat, too.

Can the van go?

No!

Jan can help.

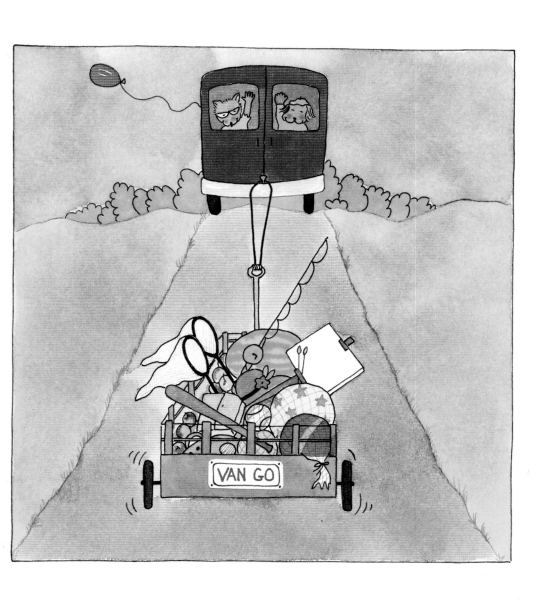

Now the van can go.

What Do You Think?

Where do you think the animals in this story are going? Why do you think that?

Make a list of the things the animals take with them on their adventure.

If you were going with them, what would you want to take? Make another list.

Pretend you and your friends will ride in a van to your favorite place. Where will you go?

What will you take with you?

What Will Happen?

You can make predictions about a story.

Use what you learn from the story and what you know from real life.

Look at these pictures.

You can use what you see and what you know. You can predict that the girl will probably take a bite of her food.

Look at these pictures. Tell what might happen next. Why do you think so?

Try This!

Look at the pictures. Draw a picture to show what you think will happen next.

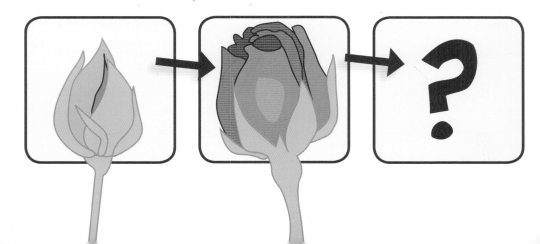

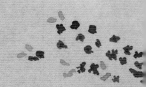

Meet the Author-Illustrator
Holly Keller

Holly Keller loves to draw animals doing things that people might do. She never had any pets growing up but says animals are more fun to draw. She gets her story ideas from things she did as a child and things her own children did. She says that children's lives are full of stories.

Requests for permission to make copies of any part of the work should be submitted online at www.harcourt.com/contact or mailed to the following address: Permissions Department, Houghton Mifflin Harcourt Publishing Company, 6277 Sea Harbor Drive, Orlando, Florida 32887-6777.

www.HarcourtBooks.com

First Green Light Readers edition 2008

Green Light Readers and its logo are trademarks of Harcourt, Inc., registered in the United States of America and/or other jurisdictions.

Library of Congress Cataloging-in-Publication Data
Keller, Holly.
The van/Holly Keller.
p. cm.
"Green Light Readers."
Summary: A family runs into difficulty when preparing for a trip in their van.
[1. Vans—Fiction.] I. Title.
PZ7.K28132Van 2008
[E]—dc22   2007042341
ISBN 978-0-15-206577-5
ISBN 978-0-15-206587-4 (pb)

A C E G H F D B
A C E G H F D B (pb)

Ages 4–6
Grade: 1
Guided Reading Level: B
Reading Recovery Level: 2

Green Light Readers
For the reader who's ready to GO!

"A must-have for any family with a beginning reader."—*Boston Sunday Herald*

"You can't go wrong with adding several copies of these terrific books to your beginning-to-read collection."—*School Library Journal*

"A winner for the beginner."—*Booklist*

Five Tips to Help Your Child Become a Great Reader

1. Get involved. Reading aloud to and with your child is just as important as encouraging your child to read independently.

2. Be curious. Ask questions about what your child is reading.

3. Make reading fun. Allow your child to pick books on subjects that interest her or him.

4. Words are everywhere—not just in books. Practice reading signs, packages, and cereal boxes with your child.

5. Set a good example. Make sure your child sees YOU reading.

Why Green Light Readers Is the Best Series for Your New Reader

● Created exclusively for beginning readers by some of the biggest and brightest names in children's books

● Reinforces the reading skills your child is learning in school

● Encourages children to read—and finish—books by themselves

● Offers extra enrichment through fun, age-appropriate activities unique to each story

● Incorporates characteristics of the Reading Recovery program used by educators

● Developed with Harcourt School Publishers and credentialed educational consultants

Daniel's Pet
Alma Flor Ada/G. Brian Karas

Sometimes
Keith Baker

A New Home
Tim Bowers

A Big Surprise
Kristi T. Butler/Pamela Paparone

Rip's Secret Spot
Kristi T. Butler/Joe Cepeda

Get Up, Rick!
F. Isabel Campoy/Bernard Adnet

Sid's Surprise
Candace Carter/Joung Un Kim

Cloudy Day Sunny Day
Donald Crews

Jan Has a Doll
Janice Earl/Tricia Tusa

Rabbit and Turtle Go to School
Lucy Floyd/Christopher Denise

The Tapping Tale
Judy Giglio/Joe Cepeda

The Big, Big Wall
Reginald Howard/Ariane Dewey/Jose Aruego

Sam and the Bag
Alison Jeffries/Dan Andreasen

The Hat
Holly Keller

The Van
Holly Keller

What I See
Holly Keller

Down on the Farm
Rita Lascaro

Big Brown Bear
David McPhail

Big Pig and Little Pig
David McPhail

Dot and Bob
David McPhail

Jack and Rick
David McPhail

Rick Is Sick
David McPhail

Best Friends
Anna Michaels/G. Brian Karas

Come Here, Tiger!
Alex Moran/Lisa Campbell Ernst

Lost!
Alex Moran/Daniel Moreton

Popcorn
Alex Moran/Betsy Everitt

Sam and Jack: Three Stories
Alex Moran/Tim Bowers

Six Silly Foxes
Alex Moran/Keith Baker

What Day Is It?
Alex Moran/Daniel Moreton

Todd's Box
Paula Sullivan/Nadine Bernard Westcott

The Picnic
David K. Williams/Laura Ovresat

Tick Tock
David K. Williams/Laura Ovresat

Look for more Green Light Readers wherever books are sold!